KNOW YOUR GAME:
Football
MARC BLOOM

SCHOLASTIC INC.
New York Toronto London Auckland Sydney

Acknowledgment

Special thanks to coach Ira Keeperman, who thrives on bringing out the best in young athletes.

About the Author

Marc Bloom writes on health, fitness, and sports for *The New York Times*, *Runner's World magazine*, *Sports Illustrated For Kids*, and other publications. He lives in Marlboro, New Jersey, with his wife and two daughters, both of whom are active in sports.

No part of this publication may be reproduced in whole or in part, or stored in a retrieval system, or transmitted in any form or by any means, electronic, mechanical, photocopying, recording, or otherwise, without written permission of the publisher. For information regarding permission, write to Scholastic Inc., 730 Broadway, New York, NY 10003.

ISBN 0-590-43312-1

Design: Brian Collins
Illustrations: Joe Taylor

Designed and produced by Peter Elek Associates,
457 Broome Street, New York, NY 10013

12 11 10 9 8 7 6 5 4 3 2 1   0 1 2 3 4 5/9
                  Printed in the U.S.A.   23

First Scholastic printing, October 1990

Contents

Introduction

Football has become one of America's most popular sports. It is played by millions of people of all ages in youth leagues, high schools, colleges, and in the professional ranks. The National Football League championship, known as the Super Bowl, draws the largest television sports audience of the year.

Football is a very exciting game for young players. It gives you a chance to work up a sweat, learn a challenging sport, play with friends, and perhaps be on a team as well.

This book will help you to enjoy football. It will explain how football is played and show you how to do your best at it.

You probably know a little about football already from watching your favorite teams on television. Maybe you've played with friends in school or are even a member of a football team.

No matter what you already know about football, there is much more to learn. And the more you know about the game, the better you'll like it.

In this book, you'll read about football skills, rules, gear, and teamwork. Most of what you read will be about tackle football. You'll also find out how to get in shape for football, how to set goals for yourself, and how to build up your confidence.

And as you'll find out, you don't have to be big to enjoy playing football. For young players, size is not important. What is important is the desire to play the game and learn all you can about it.

Chapter 1
Having Fun

Have you ever tossed a football around with a group of friends? Have you had the thrill of running for a pass, catching the ball, and racing across the field? That's what football in a team setting is like. It's an organized way to run around, play ball with friends, and have fun.

Having fun means being happy about how you and your friends play together. It also means knowing you tried your best. Doing your best shows that you're a good athlete who helps the team. Whether your team won or lost, you should be able to say to yourself, "I tried hard, and I had fun."

Football is different from most other sports in a number of ways. Most importantly, football with tackling is a contact sport. Players charge into each other as part of the game. When you block or tackle, or get tackled, you use your hands and body to make and absorb physical contact. Coaches sometimes call this "mixing it up." The pros call it "taking a hit."

This contact is new to most young players. It is natural to feel uncomfortable or afraid about it. Coaches know this and will help you get used to the rough part of the game. They teach you how to play safely and use your equipment properly so you won't get injured.

Because of the contact, some people feel football players should show how "tough" they can be. While that might be useful on the professional level, it is not necessary in youth games. Players who concentrate on the basics of the game realize that quickness and smooth-running plays are the keys to success. These players will have the most fun in football.

Another special quality of football is that every player on the field is involved in every play. Whether on offense or defense, each player has a "job" to do.

"You can't hide," says one coach. Says another, "There's no free ride."

In most other team sports, a player can take it easy at times when the action flows in another direction. In football, you're always involved in the action. This should add to your enjoyment of the game.

Football can be fun for many different reasons. These reasons include: being a member of a team, learning sportsmanship, developing skills, getting healthful exercise, and playing with rules. Also, it's fun having a coach, increasing your self-confidence, and feeling proud to wear an athletic uniform.

Being a Member of a Team

When you join a football team, you learn how to play together with kids your own age. Teamwork means thinking not only of yourself, but of what is best for the team. In football, players depend on each other for help on every play. The different positions, such as blocking and tackling, all contribute to a team's success. It is a challenge to be given a position

6

and then play it to the best of your ability.

As a member of a football team, you must attend practice sessions, pay attention to the coach, and try to learn as much as possible about the game.

Learning Sportsmanship

Have you ever helped an opposing player who fell or got hurt during a game? If you have, you've shown good sportsmanship. Even in the pros, there are examples of sportsmanship. You've probably seen a football game on TV in which one player tackles another player hard, then helps him to his feet.

Sportsmanship means being fair and thinking about the feelings of other players. Someone who is a good sport plays by the rules and understands that in a football game things don't always go the way you'd like them to.

Your coach will be proud of you if you show modesty on the field. Don't imitate the behavior of some college and pro players who do "sack dances" by jumping up and down after a tackle or throw the ball in the end zone after scoring a touchdown. This kind of showboating is immature and unsportsmanlike.

It can lead to embarrassment, too. In the 1990 Sugar Bowl, a player from the University of Alabama was embarrassed on national television. After making a tackle, the player gestured in a nasty way toward the other team. On the sidelines, his coach grabbed him by the face mask of his helmet and delivered a stern reprimand.

7

Developing Skills

For each position in football, there are many skills that are important to learn. A quarterback needs to hand the ball properly to running backs. A cornerback needs quickness in covering receivers. Most coaches will try players at many positions to see which one they play best.

Don't be disappointed if you don't get a chance to play your favorite position. As you get older and gain experience, your position may change. Even some college athletes end up playing different positions in the pros.

The way to develop skills is to be alert at all times on the field. You should also realize that you cannot learn everything at once. For example, being able to catch a pass while surrounded by defensive players is a skill that may take a while to learn. Be patient.

Getting Healthful Exercise

Football is an excellent sport for getting physically fit. You cover a lot of ground on the field when you play football. In practice and in games, you use your body to block, tackle, run, and chase after the ball.

Whether you realize it or not, all this activity is good for you. Kids, as well as adults, need exercise to be healthy. The activities you do in football will give you energy, build up your stamina, and may even help you to sleep more soundly.

When you're in shape and in good health, you

feel better, too. Your body will feel sluggish if you're not getting enough exercise.

Playing With Rules

Every sport needs rules. They are necessary for your protection and for your enjoyment of the game. Referees enforce rules.

You have to learn the rules of football and follow them, just like you learn how to catch or throw a pass. Some rules involve the way certain plays are set up and carried out. Other rules have to do with the use of gear and how a team is organized.

Having a Coach

A coach should help you learn the game and enjoy it. The coach should make you feel proud to be a member of a team and treat you with respect.

Football teams sometimes have two or three coaches. Each might have a specialty, such as working with the offense or defense. Some teams have trainers who are experienced in preventing injury and patching up scrapes.

Coaches differ in their approaches to teaching football. Some try to be gruff and tough. Others are more easygoing. Some yell; others joke around. As long as a coach treats you fair and square, you have nothing to worry about.

If, for any reason, you feel you are being mistreated by a coach, tell your parents. Parents are supposed to be involved with their kids' teams; they should be able to speak with your coach.

Increasing Self-confidence

Some people avoid football because they're afraid. They worry that they won't be good at it, or they don't like the idea of smacking into other players on the field. As you learn about the game, you'll realize almost all beginning players have the same feelings of nervousness.

And because football is a team sport, all players share in the outcome of a game. No one player should be "blamed" for a defeat, nor cheered alone for spearheading a big win.

As you gain confidence in yourself as a football player, you'll find yourself becoming a more confident person in general. Through sports, you find out how much you can achieve when you put your mind to something.

Pride in the Uniform

Football uniforms are fancy and colorful, and it is natural to feel good when you put on a fresh uniform before a game. Wearing the team colors and putting on your helmet will give you a sense of pride. You've earned it!

Seeing all your teammates suited up can get you revved up and anxious to take the field. Try your best and remember to use the skills you learned in practice.

Chapter 2
Football Rules

When you choose up sides for football games with friends, you follow a lot of rules without even realizing it. You decide how big the field will be, how many touchdowns will win the game, and whether you'll play touch or tackle football.

Rules help you understand the game, keep the activity safe, and prevent any player or team from having an unfair advantage. Imagine eight-year-olds playing against fourteen-year-olds, or one team playing the whole game with the wind at their backs.

In football, as in other sports, if you don't play by the rules you will be penalized. Referees make those decisions. They usually wear striped shirts so they are easy to spot on the field. They are called "refs" for short. They blow a whistle when a rule has been broken, and use hand signals to describe a penalty.

There are dozens of rules in football. Most youth leagues, such as Pop Warner, use NFL rules with some variations. The more you know about the rules, the better player you can become. Here are some of football's most important rules:

1. *The field:* A standard football field is 100 yards long (not counting the end zones) and 53 yards wide. Younger teams may play on smaller fields.

2. *The ball:* The ball should be made of good qual-

ity leather or rubber. The size and weight varies slightly with the level of play. (For more information on gear, see chapter 5.)

3. *Equipment and uniforms:* Helmets must be worn along with padding. Each player's jersey has a number.

4. *Blocking and tackling:* Rough play, known as "unnecessary roughness," is not allowed and results in a penalty. Examples of rough play are grabbing a player's helmet, blocking someone from behind, piling on a player who's already been tackled, and tackling the quarterback after he or she has thrown the ball.

5. *Length of periods and game:* College and pro teams play four 15-minute quarters for a total of 60 minutes. Most youth leagues play 10-to 12-minute quarters.

6. *Start of game:* Team captains meet in the middle of the field for a coin toss with the referee. The team that wins the toss decides whether to receive or kick, and which goal it will defend. The loser automatically gets first choice for the second half.

7. *Official time:* A time clock keeps game time. It runs continuously, except when plays go out-of-bounds or result in a score. It stops on incomplete passes and during time-outs.

8. *Touchdown:* Also called a TD, a touchdown scores 6 points. It is made when the offense runs with the ball or completes a pass in the defensive team's end zone.

9. *Point-after-touchdown:* After a touchdown, the scoring team gets a chance to earn another 1 or 2

points. In the pros, teams can score 1 point by place-kicking the ball from the 20-yard line through the goal-post. In Pop Warner, a point-after-touchdown is worth 2 points on a kick and 1 point on a run or pass. The youngest teams have no point-after rule and earn 7 points for a TD.

10. *Field goal:* A field goal scores 3 points. When the offensive team feels it probably won't be able to score a TD, it can try to score a field goal. This is done by kicking the ball from the team's position on the field through the goalpost of the defense.

11. *Safety:* When the team with the ball is tackled

in its own end zone, it is called a safety and the defensive squad is given 2 points.

12. *Movement of ball:* The team with the ball gets four plays ("downs") to move the ball at least 10 yards for a first down. And after you make a first down, you get another four downs to try to continue to move the ball. If the team fails, the other team gets possession of the ball.

13. *Out-of-bounds:* When a player with the ball has one foot inbounds and the other foot out-of-bounds, he or she is considered out-of-bounds.

14. *Forward passes:* Forward passes must be completed from behind the line of scrimmage, which is where the ball is placed for a hike. Once a player with the ball is past the line, he or she can toss the ball sideways or backwards, known as a lateral, but never in a forward motion.

15. *Defensive pass interference:* If a defensive player physically prevents an offensive player from having a fair chance of catching a pass (such as by shoving that player), the offensive team gets an automatic first down at the spot of the foul.

16. *Penalties:* Rules infractions, such as improper use of hands on the field, result in penalties of 5 to 15 yards, plus possible loss of down. Examples of such penalties are "holding," "personal foul," and "illegal use of hands."

17. *Fumbles:* If a player loses possession of the ball while a play is in action, it is a fumble, and any player can try to recover it.

18. *Kicks:* On a field goal attempt or point-after-

touchdown, if the ball hits the goalpost or crossbar without going through the uprights, it is not a score.

19. *Punt return:* A player waiting to catch the ball can signal for a "fair catch" by raising his or her arm. If the player catches the ball, he or she cannot run with it or be tackled. If the player drops the ball, it is considered a fumble, and anyone can reclaim it.

20. *Playing time:* Each player on a Pop Warner team must participate in at least four plays in the course of a game.

21. *Referee signals:* There are thirty-one different hand signals used by NFL refs to show a rules violation or other type of game situation. For example, for a holding penalty, the ref will put his or her right hand over the wrist of the left hand.

22. *Flag football:* In flag football, there's no tackling. To stop a player with the ball, a defensive player grabs a flag that is attached to a specially made belt worn by a player. There are usually six or eight players on a side at once, and modified blocking is permitted.

23. *Touch football:* Touch football is like flag football except flags are not used. You simply touch the player who has the ball with both hands at the same time. This style of play is also known as two-hand touch. Touch football usually is played without blocking and with as few as four players on a side at once. This is a common neighborhood game among friends. It became very popular in the early 1960s because President John F. Kennedy played touch football on the White House lawn.

Chapter 3
Football Skills

Football with tackling is easier to learn than you might think. You just have to get used to the physical contact. In most sports, you try to avoid crashing into other players. In football, you have to make that contact.

In learning football skills, you must follow directions, have the right gear on hand, and pay attention to your coach. Be aware of how other players learn the game. And remember that you cannot learn everything at once.

There are seven football skills to concentrate on. They are: 1) the three-point stance, 2) blocking, 3) tackling, 4) running with the ball, 5) catching, 6) passing, and 7) kicking.

The Three-Point Stance

The stance is how you position your body for each play. There are different stances to choose from. The most common stance, and the best one for young players, is the three-point stance. This means three parts of your body—both your feet and one hand—touch the ground as you set up for a play.

To take a three-point stance, stand with your feet apart and pointing straight ahead. Move your right foot a few inches back so the right toe is in line with

the left heel. So far, the stance is like a batting stance in baseball.

Bend your knees, crouch down, and extend your right arm in front of you with your hand touching the ground. Keep your back and right arm straight. Some players curl their fingers so their knuckles touch the ground. Rest your left arm on your left knee.

This stance should give you balance, which is crucial in football. It should also give you the ability to spring forward with leverage and power.

Be careful not to tilt your backside too high. You should not feel all your weight pressing on your right arm. As a test, you should be able to raise your right arm without falling over. If you can't, put more of your weight on your legs.

One trick is to keep your head up, looking straight ahead. If you look down, your head (and helmet) will bring your body too far forward.

To check for balance, coaches will "pop" out your right arm to see if you fall over. Practice the three-point stance on your own in front of a mirror.

This stance, or a version of it, can be used for every position except quarterback. Sometimes, running backs and receivers use a two-point stance, not leaning forward. Defensive linemen may use a four-point stance, in which both hands touch the ground. This lowers the body for greater power, but you don't have as much balance this way.

Blocking

Blocking is a way to prevent opposing players from tackling the quarterback, running back, or receiver—whoever has the ball. It involves using the body (not the hands) to push players backwards or to the side. It is done by offensive players at the line of scrimmage, in front of the quarterback (called pass

blocking), and in the open field when a runner carrying the ball has broken loose.

Whenever you block, move quickly with good balance and hit the player low, under the shoulder pads. Don't block with your helmet; slide your head to the side. Otherwise, you can hurt your neck.

On the line of scrimmage, make sure you know which player you're supposed to block. Explode from your three-point stance, moving off the ball of your left foot. Stay low; don't stand up.

Drive forward with your arms in front of you. Make your hands into fists, and bring your fists to your chest with your elbows out like wings. Push with your arms and shoulders. Take short, choppy steps.

Don't stop when you make contact. Keep driving "through" the defender so he or she will be off balance and unable to move toward the ball.

In pass blocking, you have some room in which to maneuver. Usually, you step back a few feet and help form a "pocket" or protective wall around the quarterback. Stand up, use your body more, and your legs less. If necessary, dive at the defensive player's waist to knock him or her out of the way.

Tackling

Tackling is like blocking because the object is to force the opposing player off balance. It is different because you go after the ballcarrier and are allowed to use your hands. It is part of defensive strategy.

Aim for the ballcarrier's waist. Drive your shoulder into him or her, keeping you head up and to the

19

side. Do not hit with your helmet. That's illegal—and dangerous.

When you make contact, wrap your arms around the player and pull at the knees. The player should fall down. If he or she doesn't, don't give up; keep pulling.

The bigger a ballcarrier is, the lower you'll have to aim your hit to gain leverage. At times, you may have to lunge at the ankles.

You are allowed to hand-tackle a player by grabbing his or her uniform and pulling him or her down. You're not allowed to grab the face mask of the helmet, though. And the ball is up for grabs. If you can snatch it away, you'll gain possession for your team.

Hand-tackling should be done only as a last resort. Relying on it creates bad habits. You can get hurt by reaching out for a player who's running fast.

Running with the Ball

   While the quarterback can run with the ball, most running plays are handled by two running backs, who are positioned in the backfield near the quarterback. To receive the ball from the quarterback on a running play, the back arranges his or her arms like a sandwich. One arm is across the stomach, and the other is chest high. The quarterback places the ball in between. When you feel the ball, clamp down on it, holding the ends tight with your fingertips. Remember, anybody can try to snatch it away from you.

   As you run through the players on the line of scrimmage, lean forward with your shoulders leading you. If you stand up, the ball won't be well protected. Also, you could get hit in the stomach and have the wind knocked out of you.

   If you break away from the line and into the open field, switch the ball to one arm—the arm away from the players trying to tackle you. Hold one end of the ball in your hand, the other in the crook (bend) of your elbow, or in your armpit. This allows you to pump your arms as you run.

Never run with the ball in two hands as though you were holding a basketball. Sometimes you see that kind of hotdogging on TV. But even the pros frown upon this. When you're tackled, clutch the ball again with both arms to prevent a fumble.

Run with short steps and keep your knees high. Pump your arms up and back, not side to side. Learn to fake with your hips, change directions, and follow your blockers. Once you're ahead of the defending players, don't look behind.

You are allowed to use your free arm to push tacklers away. This is known as a straight arm.

Agility is more important than speed. It's how sharply you make your moves that helps to make you an effective player. You don't have to be as fast as Carl Lewis to be a good runner in football.

Catching

Some people think you're supposed to catch a football in your chest. If you try that, the ball will probably bounce off your chest. Catch the ball with your hands, then bring it in to your body.

First you have to be in the right place to receive the ball. If you're a receiver or running back involved in a pass play, make sure you know how to run the pattern and where the ball will be thrown.

Look at the ball as it's thrown. If it comes right to you, keep your hands together and away from your

body with your thumbs touching (or pinkies if it's a low throw). If you sense you'll be tackled as soon as you make the catch, clutch the ball tightly with both arms so you won't fumble.

If the ball is thrown off to your side, you may have to reach for it with your fingertips, or even dive for the ball. Don't be fancy; be smart. Keep the defenders off guard. Don't give away all your moves.

Passing

A ball that spins through the air is called a spiral. "A spiral travels fast and is easy to catch," says Joe Montana, the all-pro quarterback who led the San Francisco 49ers to the Super Bowl championship in 1989 and 1990.

To throw a spiral, you need more than a good arm. How you stand, where you look, and how you hold the ball are just as important. This is part of setting up the pass.

23

Here's how Joe Montana does it, and how he suggests you try it, too:

• Foot position: When you receive the ball and drop back, spread your feet apart and point them toward your intended pass receiver.

If you're right-handed, your left foot is the lead leg. If you're a lefty, the right foot should lead.

Keep your weight balanced on both feet. Don't lean on one foot or stand flat-footed. Press forward on the balls on your feet.

• Head position: Point your head toward the receiver, too. Look at the receiver as much as possible.

• Hand position: When you receive the ball, hold it with both hands. Keep the ball high and pointed in the direction of your target.

• Arm position: Don't rush the pass. When you're

ready to throw, move your arm back behind your ear.
If it's a short pass, your arm won't have to go back very
far.

• The grip: Pro quarterbacks put either two or
three fingers across the laces of the ball when they
throw it. Montana uses two fingers—the pinky and fin-
ger next to it. His other fingers are placed on the side
of the ball. Use whatever grip is comfortable, but don't
let the ball lie flat in your palm. There should be a
small space between your palm and the ball.

• The throw: When you bring your arm forward to
release the ball, your elbow should pass your head
first, then your hand.

• The follow-through: Bring your hand all the
way down as you let go of the ball. Montana says,
"Your thumb should end up pointing to the ground.
That'll put spin on the ball."

Kicking

There are three kinds of kicking. One is place-
kicking for an extra point or field goal. The ball is
hiked to a player who holds the ball steady for the
kicker. Another is punting, in which the kicker re-
ceives a hike and drop-kicks the ball. Third is the kick-
off. The ball is placed upright on the field and the
kicker runs up to it and kicks off to the other team.

When kicking, keep your eye on the ball at all
times. Keep your leg stiff and meet the ball with the
top of your foot, not just your toes. Swing your leg all
the way up. Make sure the top of the ball faces up-
ward so you won't kick into the laces.

To get your leg up high, you'll need good flexibility. Make sure you do a lot of stretching exercises to stay loose. That way, your kick will have power behind it.

On a punt, stand about 10 yards behind the center, who will hike, or snap, the ball to you. Keep your arms out and hands open. Concentrate on receiving the snap. Kick in a two-step motion by leaning forward and dropping the ball gently in front of you.

On a placekick, stand in a comfortable position with your feet planted securely. Follow the ball from the center to the "holder," who sets the ball upright on the ground, holding it in place when you kick it. Keep your head down.

Kicking is one of the hardest skills for beginning players to learn. But you never know when you may be called on to kick—even in the pros. Star quarterback Randall Cunningham of the Philadelphia Eagles is the team's backup punter.

Chapter 4

Football Teamwork

Football players must work together as a team. If they don't, the team won't achieve what it set out to do, or have as much fun.

There are eleven starting spots on most tackle football teams. The coach gives each player a position. With two teams on the field at once, there are twenty-two players in action. You may be needed to play both offense and defense.

However your team is set up, the smartest thing you can do is perform your specific job, or role, on every play. That means knowing how the play will work and understanding what is expected of you. It does not mean following the action all over the field.

At almost every game, you'll hear coaches shout, "Do your job! Do your job!" In practice, the coach shows you where to position yourself on the field and what to do once play begins. During a game, many players get excited. They forget what they were taught in practice. They make the mistake of leaving their positions to do someone else's job.

The best way to move the ball up the field, or prevent the other team from doing so, is by playing as a unit. Think of a football team as a group of actors performing a play. If anyone is out of step, the performance will be mixed up. It simply won't work.

For example, a quarterback may be a terrific passer, but if the players on the line of scrimmage do not block successfully, he or she won't get off the pass.

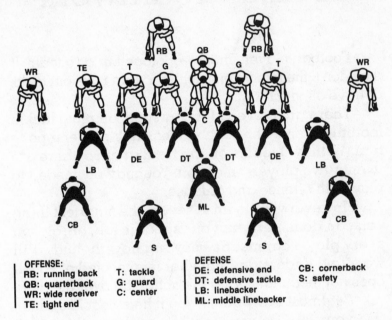

OFFENSE:
RB: running back
QB: quarterback
WR: wide receiver
TE: tight end
T: tackle
G: guard
C: center

DEFENSE
DE: defensive end
DT: defensive tackle
LB: linebacker
ML: middle linebacker
CB: cornerback
S: safety

In addition to the quarterback, the other offensive positions are: center, guard, tackle, wide receiver, tight end, running back, and kicker. The defensive positions are: defensive tackle and end, linebacker, cornerback, and safety.

There are many different ways to set up a team on the field. This is known as the team's formation. You've probably heard of "split," "wing," and "I" formations from listening to football announcers on television.

You'll find that a coach will use different systems in the way he or she sets up positions. You should know what each player is supposed to do, and how all the different players work together.

OFFENSE
Center

The main job of the center is to hike the ball to the quarterback. Stand over the ball with your feet spread apart. Place both hands on the ball. One hand, the right, should be used to snap the ball; the left is for balance and should not exert any pressure. Keep your head up but make sure your eyes are on the ball.

Each snap of the ball has a signal, usually a number. In the huddle between plays, the quarterback says what the signal will be. When the players take their positions, the quarterback calls a series of num-

bers out loud for everyone to hear. When he or she gets to the signal, the ball is snapped.

Snap the ball between your legs into the quarterback's hands. Centers also block. Once the hike is made, move right into your blocking assignment.

On most plays, the quarterback will be standing right behind you with his hands underneath your rear. When the quarterback is positioned several yards back, in order to set up the pass as quickly as possible, you'll have to hike for distance. The same is true when hiking to punters. It also applies to holders for placekickers.

Guard and Tackle

There are usually two guards and two tackles on the front line. They are known as offensive linemen. They block to protect the passer from being tackled, or open holes for running backs to run through. They should be persistent and agile.

If a play calls for a run up the middle, the lineman must work in a small area to clear the way. If there's a pass, the lineman may play a little looser since players will be more spread out. On a run to the outside, sometimes called a sweep, the linemen have to be quick enough to dart from their positions and block for a running back sweeping to the far side of the field.

Wide Receiver

Wide receivers need "good hands." They should also be quick enough to get away from defensive players. Wide receivers are also known as split ends because they line up far to the side on the line of scrimmage.

The best receivers, like Jerry Rice of the San Francisco 49ers, develop a feel for where the ball is thrown. Even if a ball is not thrown perfectly, a good receiver can use his or her "radar" to go after it and snag it.

Receivers also learn to vary the way they dash downfield to be in position to catch a pass. How a receiver runs when a play begins is called a pass pattern. There are names for each pattern, like post pattern or down-and-out. Throw a couple of fakes into your pattern to get clear.

Never give up on the ball. Even if it seems out of reach, try to tip it so the defense won't intercept it.

Tight End

Tight ends block on running plays and are used as receivers for short yardage on pass plays. Tight ends typically catch the ball in heavy traffic. They must be able to hold onto the ball even when tackled hard by two or three defenders at once.

Running Back

Not long ago, running backs were called fullbacks and halfbacks. Now they're called backs or wings.

Teams usually have two backs set behind the quarterback. These three players make up the backfield. They work together. Backs are given handoffs and pitchouts on running plays, and are sometimes needed to receive passes. They also help block for the quarterback.

Backs need to be good all-around athletes. They must be able to receive the ball cleanly on running plays and protect the ball as they run and get tackled. Backs must also learn the different ways to cut through the line, dodge and shake off tacklers, and run for long yardage in the open field.

Kicker

In the pros, teams have specialists who do nothing but kick. One specialist will be a punter, while another will be a placekicker. They can sail the ball 50 or 60 yards in the air.

In youth football, any player can also serve as a kicker. Kicking for distance and accuracy is considered a difficult skill. That's why in Pop Warner leagues a kick after a TD is worth 2 points instead of 1.

Kickers have to learn a combination of skills. They also need to relax under pressure. They can't get nervous and tense up as defensive players charge toward them.

Quarterback

The quarterback is known as the "field general." Every play (except for kicks) starts with the quarterback calling the signals, receiving the ball, and setting the play in motion. A team with a smart, reliable quarterback usually will do very well.

Other players tend to look up to the quarterback as a team leader. Quarterbacks should be able to accept this role and encourage teammates to practice hard, learn the game, and try their best.

Having a great arm is not the most important part of a quarterback's game. He or she must be the team's expert on how all the plays work. The quarterback must be able to think fast and make quick decisions in the middle of plays.

For example, if the receivers are covered tightly on a pass play, the quarterback must decide whether to throw the ball out-of-bounds, run with the ball himself, or "eat the ball" by dropping to the ground with it before risking a hard tackle. The decision will be based on the score, field position, how much time is left, and whether he feels he can gain yardage by running. The quarterback has about five seconds to figure all this out.

In youth football, most plays are running plays. It's easier to make a handoff and gain a few yards, than to complete a pass. Even so, on handoffs, quarterbacks must be able to plant the ball precisely into the arms of backs.

Most quarterbacks, even in college and the pros, do not decide which plays to use. The coach decides the play. He or she signals the quarterback from the sidelines, or sends the play in with a substitute who tells the quarterback what it is.

Of course, passing cannot be forgotten. (See chapter 3 for the passing advice of Super Bowl hero Joe Montana.) Good, crisp passing, even for short gains, keeps the defense on guard and makes it easier for running backs to find holes.

DEFENSE
Defensive Tackle and End

The tackles and ends form the defensive line. Usually, there are two of each, creating a four-person line.

Every player on the line tries to stop running plays, or rushes the quarterback on a pass play. They use quickness, agility, and sometimes power to out-maneuver the offense. They try to be in a position to tackle whoever has the ball.

Linemen cannot get fooled by the quarterback's slick fakes. They cannot give up pursuit of the ball. They should try to cause fumbles, then pounce on the loose ball.

Linebacker

Linebackers form the middle row of the defense. There are usually two outside linebackers and a middle linebacker, who may be considered the defensive leader. He or she gives instructions to other players, like a "defensive quarterback."

Linebackers stop running backs who make it through the line. They also defend against short passes. They must react quickly to whether a play is a run or a pass. Wise linebackers get to know the habits of quarterbacks and can tell pretty quickly how a play might work.

If linebackers detect a pass play, they might rush through the line to try and smother the quarterback. This is known as a blitz.

Cornerback

Cornerbacks guard the wide receivers. They try to prevent passes from being completed. They stick like glue to receivers and sometimes have the chance to intercept a pass.

Cornerbacks must be able to change directions quickly. Receivers do a lot of faking, so cornerbacks try not to get faked out. They learn whether to play tight or loose against certain receivers.

Cornerbacks block passes with their hands or bodies. They also have to tackle. If a receiver catches a pass, he or she has to be stopped. If the receiver races away with the ball, the cornerback has to run the receiver down and maybe dive to make a tackle that would prevent a touchdown.

Safety

Two safeties make up the defensive backfield, or secondary. They play deep, sometimes close to the goal line. They cover running backs and receivers who break away from the rest of the defense and head for a touchdown.

They must be capable of covering a wide area of the field. They defend against long passes and also tackle backs motoring at full speed toward the goal.

Sometimes, one safety is called the free safety and the other the strong safety. The strong safety may have specific players to watch, while the free safety is assigned to roam around, responding to how a play develops.

Chapter 5

Football Gear

There's probably more gear in football than in any other sport. Maybe you've seen films of professional players suiting up for a game. Have you noticed how many articles of clothing there are, and how each area of the body gets protected?

If you play on your own with friends, all you need is a football. If you play tackle, you should have a helmet, too. In an organized league, however, you'll be required to wear padding and other protective gear. It will be necessary in practices as well as in games.

A lot of the gear will be loaned to you by the team. You may have to purchase certain items in sporting goods stores.

Football: The best ones are made of leather or hard rubber. They vary in size and weight, with the slightly smaller and lighter balls for young players. If you're on a team, you should still have a ball for practicing on your own. Buy a rubber ball. Leather balls may get scraped up on hard surfaces.

Helmet: The helmet is your most important piece of equipment. It has thick foam padding to cushion your head against contact. Some of the newer models come with a device that pumps air into the padding for added protection. Helmets are expensive, and teams usually provide them.

If you buy your own, make sure it comes with a face mask and chin strap. Also make sure it has a label assuring it has met national safety standards. The seal reads: NOCSAE.

Shoes: At first, it's fine to play in your regular, everyday sneakers. But make sure the sneakers are sturdy. If they're worn out, you could end up hurting your foot. High-tops provide the best support.

As you improve your play, you'll need to purchase shoes better suited for football. These are called cleats. They are usually black and made of leather. On the bottom, they have thick nubs that give you traction when you run.

Since tackle football is played on grass, good traction is important. Games are played in the rain on wet fields. If you wear sneakers, you may slip and fall.

There are special cleats for football, but those

shoes are not necessary for beginning players. Obtain soccer cleats instead. You'll ruin your cleats if you walk around in them, or use them for other sports played on concrete surfaces.

After a game, your cleats will be dirty and may be caked with mud. Clean your cleats and keep them dry. Make sure they're clean on the inside, too.

Teams won't provide shoes. You'll have to buy them.

Padding: There are shoulder pads, as well as hip pads, knee pads, and thigh pads. They fit underneath your jersey and pants. Some teams also require rib pads and "tail" pads for your backside.

Uniform: The clothing part of the uniform consists of a shirt (also called a jersey), pants, shorts, and socks. There are different types of jerseys, such as T-shirts and those with three-quarter sleeves. The pants fit snugly and come down to the knees. Shorts are standard athletic wear. The socks are long and thick.

Uniforms have numbers on them. Usually, the numbers are based on which position you play. For example, quarterbacks are given low numbers (1–19), while defensive linemen are given high numbers (90–99).

Keep your uniform fresh and clean.

Other protective wear: Leagues may require a mouthpiece to protect your teeth. They attach to the face mask of your helmet. Boys must wear a jockstrap and "cup" for the groin. More experienced players may be taped around the hands and feet just like the pros for maximum protection.

Safety rules: All jewelry must be removed before a game. That includes watches, rings, earrings, and necklaces. Eyeglasses and contact lenses can be worn but must be of non-breakable glass or protected by outer safety glasses strapped around the head. Playing with any sharp object on your body or clothes can hurt others, or cause yourself harm.

Water bottles: To feel refreshed, always take a plastic water bottle to practices and games. Fill it with cold water and ice or a sports drink. This is absolutely necessary in warm weather, but it's a good idea even when it's cool. In football, running around builds up a keen thirst. If you don't drink water after sweating, you can get sick.

Getting dressed: At times, it may seem like dressing for a game takes longer than the game itself. Here's how it works: First you put on your jockstrap, then your cup over it (for boys). Your shorts come next, and then your socks. After that, attach the knee pads and thigh pads. Then, you fit on a "girdle" that contains the hip pads and tail pads. Finally, your pants go on.

Now it's time for your upper body. Put on your shoulder pads and rib pads if you have them. Then slip on your jersey. Put in your mouthpiece. All that's left are your helmet and shoes.

Now you're all set to play football.

Chapter 6
Football Conditioning

Your greatest foe on the football field is not a player on the opposing team. It's fatigue. Once you get tired, you're likely to let up and not try as hard. Coaches call this "giving up" on a play.

When you give up on plays, you not only hurt your team's chances of winning but you increase your own risk of injury. A player who's tired does not use correct technique or concentrate on his or her job. He or she is not alert on the field.

If you feel exhausted when blocking, tackling, or running with the ball, opposing players will have an advantage over you. Your strength will be sapped, and your muscles will be weak. You'll get hit more often, and when you do you'll bruise more easily.

In a way, you'll be cheating yourself. All the skills you've learned won't be worth much. You'll be too tired to use them.

Even the best athletes need to work at being in shape. That's why the pros have training camps prior to the regular season. All ball players need to limber up, work their muscles, and perhaps even lose some weight in order to block, tackle, throw, catch, pass, run, kick—do whatever is needed on a football field.

Have you ever gotten out of breath while playing sports? Have you ever run down a field and felt your lungs ready to burst? Athletes young and old experience these feelings at one time or another. They are part of the process of getting in shape.

As you condition yourself, you improve your physical fitness. Your muscles become stronger. You'll breathe easier when you run hard. You'll gain quickness, too, which is very important in football.

Fitness takes time. It can't happen in one day or one week. Be patient. Don't overdo it. Making progress at a gradual pace brings the best results.

In football, players often collide. You dive for a ball, change directions quickly, and play on muddy fields. A well-conditioned player will be less likely to get hurt.

If you're just learning the game, conditioning can help you make up for lack of skills. If you can hustle, you'll outplay your opponents. You'll also last longer as the game wears on. Coaches like to see players show just as much pep in the fourth quarter as in the first.

Being in shape for football is a year-round responsibility. Pre-season training should not be a time to begin getting in shape. You should already be in pretty good shape from other sports. Soccer, running, bicycling, and swimming are some activities that will keep you fit if you do them regularly. Basketball is excellent, too, as long as you move around a lot on the court.

When you get together with your team and coaches, you'll do many conditioning drills, just like they do at Notre Dame and other top college teams.

The Notre Dame coach, Lou Holtz, has a drill he calls "gassers."

He has his players sprint—run as fast as they can—from sideline to sideline, across the field. That's a distance of about 50 yards. They might do this ten or twenty times. Holtz calls those drills gassers because if you can't do them, you've run out of gas.

Sprints (sometimes called "wind sprints") are hard, but during a tough game you'll be glad you did them. In football, you do a lot of fast running with little chance to rest.

One favorite drill of coaches is for players to sprint one way, do a somersault, then sprint the other way. Another drill is called "crabbing." You get down on all fours and "run" with your hands and feet like claws on the ground.

Then there's the "carioca" drill, used to develop coordination and running. You run sideways, crossing one leg over the next as though on a dance line. In football, there's a lot of sideways (or lateral) movement. This drill causes many players to trip over their own feet. It's a lot of fun, and after a while you'll get it right.

There are many drills you can do on your own, or with a few friends. All you need is a football and a little space. One player hikes the ball to a quarterback while the third player races downfield to catch a pass. Take turns throwing, hiking, and running.

Conditioning is so important to the pros that some teams hire experts to give the players advice. One expert who has worked with NFL teams is Steve

Williams, a former record-breaking sprinter. He watches players run, then gives each a report card on how they do. Follow some of his advice, and your running will eventually earn you straight A's:

1. Always run on your toes. Running flat-footed slows you down and increases your chance of injury.

2. Pump your arms. Move them up and back (not side to side), keeping them close to your body.

3. For practice, do sprints while carrying a light weight or rock in your hands. When you run without the weight, you'll feel lighter and faster.

4. Do some stop-and-go running like you do in a game. For example, run fast (not all out) for 30 yards, stop, turn around, then run back at top speed.

5. Jump rope. This teaches you to run on your toes and also develops coordination, leg strength, and endurance. Try it for ten or fifteen minutes at a time. Make sure you land on your toes and keep your knees bent. Do it on soft surfaces and wear cushiony shoes.

The fast running in football puts a lot of pressure on the upper front leg muscles, called the quadriceps. When you run fast, you lift your knees high; the "quads" support the knee and fatigue quickly if they're not strong.

To strengthen the quadriceps, try hopping back and forth over a short bench. Do this for twenty seconds, then rest. Then hop for thirty seconds, rest; hop for forty-five seconds, then a minute. If a bench is too high, simply hop over a football.

As you work the legs, you may find your stomach is weak. Experienced athletes have learned that each part of the body affects another part. A soft belly will slow you down. Sit-ups will strengten your stomach, though. Try to do 25–50 sit-ups every day. Do them slowly, keeping your knees bent.

All-Pro running back Herschel Walker of the Minnesota Vikings does 1,500 sit-ups and several hundred push-ups every day. He also does weight training, as do most college and pro players, but feels young players should not work out with weights until they're at least sixteen or seventeen. Most coaches and sports medicine experts agree. Instead, for strength, do push-ups, pull-ups, and chin-ups. Or improvise. Find a rubber cord (like the kind used to tie luggage) and attach it to a doorknob. By stretching the cord back and forth (with the door closed), you can develop arm strength.

Remember, if you get tired during a game, your skills will be wasted. Imagine trying to race for a pass or tackle a running back when your legs are caving in. Or think of fighting for the ball when you feel like you need a nap.

The more your physical fitness improves, the less you'll experience the most embarrassing feeling of all in football: giving up on a play.

Chapter 7

Football Organization and Stars

The first football game was played on November 6, 1869, in New Brunswick, New Jersey. It was a college game between Rutgers and Princeton, and it was quite different from how football is played today. In many ways, it was more like a soccer game. There was no passing, and one point was awarded for each ball kicked over the goal line. Princeton won, 8–0.

Football developed in the eastern part of the U.S., and by the early 1900s large crowds packed college stadiums to watch games. A famous coach from that era, Amos Alonzo Stagg of the University of Chicago, created a style of play that has been in use ever since. This includes the forward pass, huddle, T-formation, even uniform numbers.

Pro football also began to be popular at this time. One player who made headlines was Jim Thorpe. He was a track star who won two gold medals in the 1912 Olympic Games. Thorpe also could fly on the gridiron (another term for football field) and starred for a team from Ohio, the Canton Bulldogs. Thorpe was paid $250 per game.

What eventually became the National Football League was started in 1920. Thorpe was the league's first president.

The NFL was not very successful in those days.

College football received more attention. The 1924 Notre Dame team inspired one of football's most famous nicknames—the Four Horsemen.

The name was coined by a sportswriter, Grantland Rice, and it referred to the Notre Dame backfield: Harry Stuhldreher, Don Miller, Jim Crowley, and Elmer Layden. When Notre Dame defeated Army in a big game in New York, Rice wrote, "Outlined against a blue-gray October sky, the Four Horsemen rode again . . ."

Notre Dame was involved in another historic incident. Its star player back in 1920 had been a halfback named George Gipp. Players did not always specialize then, and Gipp was known as a triple threat—someone who could run, pass, and punt. That very year, however, Gipp died tragically of pneumonia.

Before Gipp died, he told the Notre Dame coach, Knute Rockne, to ask the team to "win one for the Gipper." In 1928, before another big game with Army, Rockne told this to his squad. And Notre Dame won, 12–6.

It was not until the 1960s that pro football would really flourish. The main reason was the Super Bowl, which matched the winning teams from the National Football League and American Football League (a new group that started in 1959).

The first Super Bowl was played in 1967, as a finale to the '66 season. Led by quarterback Bart Starr, the Green Bay Packers of the NFL defeated the Kansas City Chiefs of the AFL, 35–10.

47

Suddenly the television networks became very interested in football. The fast pace of the game seemed to attract viewers at home. As the TV audience grew, many superstars were created and salaries increased.

One star from the sixties was quarterback Joe Namath, who shocked the sports world when he signed a contract out of college with the New York Jets for $427,000. Today, the average player makes more than that in a single season.

All this interest led in 1970 to the weekly television broadcast of *Monday Night Football*. Sports fans could now watch football not just on weekends.

The Super Bowl is now seen on TV by over 100 million Americans. The game is seen live or on tape in sixty foreign countries.

This amazing popularity has generated football growth in all levels of the game. These are the different branches of the sport:

Youth Leagues

Youth leagues for young players exist in most communities throughout the country. They may be part of town recreation programs or part of a national organization, such as Pop Warner Football. Pop Warner leagues are for players aged seven to fifteen.

High School

Most high schools have football teams. In many towns across the country, the high school game is the major sports event of the week. There are pep rallies and parades, along with entertaining halftime shows.

48

Games are written up in the area's newspapers, and top players become local heroes. Some players are good enough to earn scholarships to play football in college. High school programs come under the guidelines of the National Federation of State High School Athletic Associations. They are ranked nationally by the newspaper *USA Today*.

College

Most colleges have football teams. At some schools, football is considered the most important sport. Football stadiums are filled to capacity on fall Saturdays, earning a lot of money in ticket sales for the schools. Colleges also are paid large sums whenever their games are on TV. The best college players are "drafted" by the pros, and many go on to successful careers in the NFL.

The goal of major college teams is to be invited to a bowl game at the end of the season. Bowl games serve as college championships and help determine the final rankings of teams. The leading bowl games are the Rose Bowl, Cotton Bowl, Orange Bowl, and Sugar Bowl. Traditionally these four games are played on New Year's Day.

The Pros

The two wings of the National Football League are now called the National Football Conference (NFC) and American Football Conference (AFC). Each conference has 14 teams for a total of 28 NFL squads. They play sixteen regular-season games. Qualifying

49

teams go on to the play-offs, which lead to the Super
Bowl. There also is a Pro Bowl game made up of NFL
All-Stars.

Each NFL team has a roster of 45 players. There
are 1,260 NFL players in all.

Pro Football Stars

Following are some of the game's greatest players, past and present.

• Stars of the Past

Jim Thorpe: Running back who starred for several
teams in the early 1900s and was a track-and-field
gold medalist in the 1912 Olympic Games. He is considered one of the greatest all-around athletes ever.

Sammy Baugh: Quarterback and punter who
played for the Washington Redskins from 1937 to 1952.
Known as "Slinging" Sammy Baugh for his great
passing arm.

George Blanda: Quarterback and kicker who
played a record 26 seasons, from 1949 to 1975. He holds
the all-time scoring record. When he finally retired, he
was forty-eight years old!

Johnny Unitas: Quarterback for the Baltimore
Colts from 1956 to 1972. He set numerous NFL passing
records and led them to the Super Bowl title in 1971.

Jim Brown: Considered the greatest running back
ever, he played for the Cleveland Browns from 1957 to
1965 and holds the all-time record for most touchdowns scored (126). He became an actor and had roles
in many films including *The Dirty Dozen.*

Joe Namath: Quarterback for the New York Jets

from 1965 to 1976. He was known as "Broadway Joe" for his late-night party-going.

O.J. Simpson: Running back who played from 1969 to 1979 for the Buffalo Bills and San Francisco 49ers. Now a member of the announcing crew for *Monday Night Football,* he has also been seen in a number of TV commercials.

• Stars of the Present

Eric Dickerson, Indianapolis Colts: Running back who has rushed for over 1,000 yards seven straight years, has led the league in rushing four times, and is seventh all-time in rushing yardage.

Boomer Esiason, Cincinnati Bengals: Quarterback who led the AFC in passing for 1989 and was rated second only to Joe Montana in the entire NFL. He was the NFL passing leader in 1988.

Dan Marino, Miami Dolphins: Quarterback who holds the all-time NFL record for passing yardage in a single season, over 5,000 yards in 1984.

Joe Montana, San Francisco 49ers: The best quarterback in the game today and considered one of the greatest ever. He has starred in three Super Bowl triumphs for the 49ers and completed an amazing 70 percent of his passes during the 1989 season.

Jerry Rice, San Francisco 49ers: Wide receiver who is Joe Montana's favorite target. He caught key passes in the 49ers' Super Bowl wins and was the NFL scoring leader in 1987.

Barry Sanders, Detroit Lions: The latest NFL star, this running back led the league in rushing in 1989, earning Rookie-of-the-Year honors.

Chapter 8
Training Rules

Getting into shape requires time, effort, and sweat. Getting out of shape happens a lot faster. If you do no physical activity for a week or two, you'll find this out. You'll probably feel tired, weak, slow, and eventually when you go back to play sports your ability will suffer.

That's why most athletes, including football players, participate in several different sports year-round. They might run or swim or ride a bicycle. Or, they might play some basketball or tennis.

Good athletes like to keep their bodies tuned up. They know that the first rule of sports is: Use it or lose it. Any part of your body that you do not use regularly becomes weak.

There are many rules for building your body for sports, staying in shape, and preventing injury. Being aware of them will help you in football and other sports as well.

1. *Shape up:* During the football season, when you're practicing and playing games regularly, you probably don't need to do much extra exercise. When you're not playing in season, try to run or bicycle or swim a couple of times a week, and also do some stretching exercises.

2. *Enjoy sports:* Pick activities that you enjoy so

that you can look forward to doing them.

3. *Variety is best:* Even if football is your favorite, try other sports, too, so you won't get bored. Many adults who exercise now vary their activities. One day they run; the next day they might swim or bike. This is known as "cross-training."

One pro football player who benefits from cross-training is Bo Jackson, a major league baseball star as well. Jackson has been featured in a Nike commercial that showed his talents in many sports. When it comes to training, Bo knows what works.

4. *Dress properly:* When it's cold, wear an extra jersey or sweatshirt. Have a hat and gloves ready. In the heat, wear light colors, which are cooler than dark because they don't absorb the heat.

5. *Eat properly:* Your diet can affect how you feel during a game. For more on eating for sports, see chapter 9.

6. *Get enough rest:* Young athletes need plenty of sleep at night. If you have difficulty sleeping, make sure you tell your parents.

Rest involves more than sleep, though; it also means taking a break from hard exercise. It's not healthy to play hard day after day. Even the pros take days off.

7. *Be patient:* Getting in shape is a kind of education for your body. Just like you can't become a whiz in science overnight, you can't develop your body in a short time, either.

8. *Be specific:* Your body gets in shape in specific ways. For example, your legs are strengthened by

running, but not all running is the same. For football, fast running is better than slow running because your movement on the field is in quick bursts.

9. *Warm up:* Always warm up before playing by jogging, stretching, and throwing the ball around. This will loosen you up.

10. *Cool down:* After a game, everyone usually rushes away. If necessary, "cool down" on your own with more stretching. Your muscles will appreciate this the next day.

11. *Don't skimp on drinks:* Always take a water bottle to practices and games. Drink before the game, between quarters, and after the game. You sweat in the cold as well as in the heat, so you must drink even when it's cold out.

A wise coach will allow you to drink as much as you want. There may be some coaches who prohibit players from drinking as a way of punishing those who may not be following instructions. This is wrong. If it happens to you, tell your parents, who may need to discuss this with your coach.

12. *Getting strong:* As you increase physical fitness, you build strong muscles. In most sports, including football, quickness and the intelligent use of your body are more important than power. To build extra strength, do exercises like push-ups and sit-ups. At your age, weight training is not necessary.

Chapter 9
Good Food

There are two mistaken beliefs about eating for football. Number 1: You have to eat a lot. Number 2: You have to eat a lot of meat—maybe even a thick steak before a big game.

For football, or any sport, you don't have to eat a lot of anything—especially meat. But old ideas die hard. Some people still believe in stuffing themselves with beef. They think it'll make them stronger. Baloney.

These ideas remain because of what is seen in the pros. Many pro football players are very big, standing well over 6 feet and weighing over 250 pounds. Players like William "The Refrigerator" Perry of the Chicago Bears brag about the huge amount of food they eat. Well, if you were 6'6" and over 300 pounds, you'd have to eat a lot, too.

So, the first rule of eating for football is: If you're not 6'6" and over 300 pounds, you don't have to eat any more than you usually do.

The second rule is: Eat as little fat as possible. Meat is high in fat, so try not to eat meat every day. It'll only make you heavy. And you won't feel right.

Fat in foods slows you down and clogs your system. It makes you feel weak and tired. As an athlete, you have to zip around like a sports car. Your body is like an engine: It needs fuel. Fat is an example of the wrong kind of fuel.

Fat is found in large amounts of "fast" foods. The meals that you eat at roadside burger restaurants are high in fats.

Did you know that many of the foods that you enjoy eating are really very good for you as a young football player? Does your mouth water at the thought of a pizza pie? If so, you'll be glad to know that pizza is a meal that is not only enjoyable but also healthy. Foods that are good for you don't have to taste bad.

You've probably heard the phrase "balanced diet." Milk, bread, meat, fish, fruits, and vegetables are some foods that go into a balanced diet. You'd feel pretty awful if you ate only one kind of food all the time. Many people assume that foods like pizza are not good for you. That is because they put toppings like sausage and pepperoni on their pizza. Plain pizza usually is made of cheese, tomato sauce, and dough. There's nothing unhealthy about that. If you put vegetables like pepper or mushroom on your pizza, that's okay, too. However, sausage and pepperoni have a lot of fat in them.

The third rule of eating for football is: Plan ahead. If you don't plan ahead, you could wind up with a side pain during a football game. You've probably felt this type of pain during sports. It's known as a "stitch." Eating too close to a game can cause this to happen. So can eating fatty foods that are not easily digested. If you eat burgers and fries right before a game, you may feel like a "blob."

Top athletes know this and make sure they know when practices and games are scheduled. It's a good idea to eat at least two hours before exercise.

During the week, when you attend school, your sports activities are held late in the afternoon or evening. At this time, your breakfast and lunch are most important. On weekends, when play may be held in the morning, your dinner the night before and breakfast that day—if you have one—become crucial.

Should you eat the morning of a game? Only if you finish eating at least two hours before play. Get up early. Have a light breakfast, such as a nutritional cereal with skim milk and sliced banana, muffins, fruit, or yogurt.

For sports, just about the best food you can eat is probably one of your favorites: spaghetti. Spaghetti, ziti, and other noodle dishes are all types of pasta.

Pasta is a high-performance fuel for your body. It contains almost no fat but plenty of carbohydrates. Your muscles love carbohydrates. They devour them for energy.

Some people think spaghetti is a fattening food. It is if you drown it in fatty toppings. Tomato sauce is best. Go easy on the meatballs and sausage.

As you can guess, the fourth rule of eating for sports is: When in doubt, stick with pasta.

You've seen that many different types of foods are good for you, and good-tasting, too. This leads to the fifth and final rule: Eat a variety of foods. No food—even a Big Mac or a Whopper—is totally "bad" for you as long as you don't make a habit of it.

Chapter 10

Setting Goals

When you watch a football game on TV, oftentimes you see sports reporters asking top players about their goals for the upcoming season. Whether it's Eric Dickerson or Lawrence Taylor, each athlete has specific goals in mind.

Pros do not always like to reveal their goals. Some of the players and coaches feel it could inspire other teams to make plans to beat them.

If you keep your goals high, you could surprise yourself. That's what happened to high school placekicker Kevin Knope of Greece, New York, in 1989. His coach at Olympia High School, George Giordano, called him over before a game with Arcadia High. Giordano told Knope that he might have a chance to tie the national high school record of kicking five field goals in a single game.

Knope's reaction? "Let's go for seven," he said.

The result? Knope kicked seven field goals to set a new record, and his team won, 41–0.

A goal is something you'd like to achieve. You probably have goals all the time that may involve friends, family, or school. When you study for a test or save money to buy a friend a birthday present, you certainly have goals in mind.

Some goals are short-term and may be a few

weeks away. Others are long-term and may be months or even years into the future. It's good to have both kinds of goals.

Why You Need Goals

If you play sports with goals, you'll gain an advantage. For example, in football, one of the first skills you learn is blocking. At first, blocking an opposing player won't be that easy. If you set for yourself the goal of learning the proper blocking stance and practice that, you'll become an effective blocker.

Determining Your Goals

Success in sports is almost guaranteed as long your goals are realistic. If you're put at cornerback, don't think, "I'm going to get a lot of interceptions." Tell yourself this, instead: "I'm going to learn how to block passes the best I can."

Take your main goals and approach them one step at a time. In pass defense, you have to stick to the receiver, keep your eyes on the ball, not be fooled by fakes, and time your attempt to smack the ball away when it's thrown. A sensible goal to begin with would be to learn how to stay close to the receiver when he or she runs a pass pattern.

Your goals must be geared to your age, experience, and the time you have to put into a sport. Choose short-term goals that are realistic and encourage you to progress from week to week. Choose long-term goals that keep you motivated, and don't make demands on yourself that are impossible to live up to.

Achieving Your Goals

In college and pro football, success is not based on physical ability alone. All players study the game in football "classes." They review films of previous games, jotting down notes, and learn set plays that the coaches teach.

Players keep this information in a handy notebook so they can make sure they've learned their lessons well. "Our coach says that each game is like a final exam," said top quarterback Boomer Esiason of the Cincinnati Bengals, in an article in *Sports Illustrated For Kids.* "You want to study and be prepared because then you are confident, and you can't wait to take the exam."

You should do this, too. Take a notebook and make it into a football diary. Design it like a calendar, and write down the details of practices and games so you'll be able to keep track of your progress. You can also write down anything funny or unusual that may have happened.

Direct your goals toward yourself. If you focus on beating or outplaying someone, you may become frustrated, since you can't determine another person's efforts. Concentrate on what you yourself can do to improve.

Don't be shy about asking others for help. Parents, teachers, coaches, teammates, and sports doctors can be called on for advice and encouragement.

Be patient. Always keep your most important goals in mind.

Glossary
Football Talk

You've learned a lot of new words, names, and phrases that are part of the language of football. Here's a summary of key terms, in alphabetical order. Try to know them all.

backfield: the quarterback and running backs, who are set up behind the line of scrimmage

blitz: when linebackers charge through the defensive line to rush the quarterback

blocking: using your arms and body to prevent a defensive player from reaching the player with the ball

bowl games: post-season championships for leading college teams

center: offensive player who hikes the ball to the quarterback

cleats: hard shoes with grooves on the bottom to give you traction on soft fields

cool-down: easy exercise to relax your body after a practice or game

cornerback: defensive player who tries to prevent wide receivers from catching passes

cross-training: participating in different sports to get into the best possible shape

defense: the players trying to prevent the team with the ball from scoring

end zone: the area of the field past the goal line where touchdowns are scored

fair catch: when a player signals to receive a punt without running with the ball

field goal: when a ball is kicked through the goal post for a 3-point score

first down: when a team moves the ball at least 10 yards on a play, or on a series of two, three, or four plays

flag football: a form of touch football in which a player with the ball is stopped by grabbing a flag from his or her waist

formation: how a team lines up for a play

forward pass: a pass thrown by a quarterback (or running back) from behind the line of scrimmage to a player past the line

fumble: when a player carrying the ball loses possession of it, leaving the ball up for grabs

gridiron: another term for football field

helmet: important protection for your head during practices and games

huddle: when a team gathers after each play to plan the next play

interception: when a pass is "picked off" by a defensive player, giving that player's team possession of the ball

lateral: a pass made in a backwards or sideways direction

linebacker: players who form the middle of a defensive unit and cover both running and passing plays

offense: the team that has the ball and is trying to score

pads: protection for the shoulders and other parts of the body, worn during practices and games

pass interference: when a defensive player unfairly prevents a receiver from catching a pass, resulting in a penalty

pass pattern: the way a receiver runs down field to be in position to catch a pass

penalty: punishment for rule violations resulting in loss of yardage

physical fitness: being in shape to play the game

placekicker: player who specializes in kicking field goals

point-after-touchdown: a run, pass, or kick that is worth 1 or 2 points after a touchdown is made

Pop Warner Football: a league for young players that exists in many communities throughout the country

punt: a kick by the offensive team to the defensive team, when the offense is unable to move the ball

quarterback: the "field general" who controls almost every play by running, passing, and making handoffs to running backs

referees: the officials in charge of the game

running back: players who run with the ball, sometimes block, and also catch passes

safety: 1) defensive players who cover deep runs and passes, 2) also a 2-point play in which the offense is tackled behind its own goal

spiral: a pass that spins smoothly through the air

straight arm: a runner using the arm without the ball to push tacklers away

Super Bowl: the championship game of the National Football League

sweep: a running play that goes around the far side of the field

tackling: when a defensive player tries to bring a player with the ball to the ground

tight end: an offensive player who blocks and catches short passes

three-point stance: setting up for a play with the right hand on the ground and the left hand resting on your left leg

touchdown: a run or pass over the goal line that is worth 6 points

touch football: football without tackling in which a player carrying the ball is stopped by touching him or her with two hands (also called two-hand touch)

warm-up: exercise to loosen up before practice or a game

wide receiver: offensive player whose main role is to catch passes

Appendix

NATIONAL FOOTBALL LEAGUE TEAMS

National Football Conference (NFC)

Eastern Division:
Dallas Cowboys
New York Giants
Philadelphia Eagles
Phoenix Cardinals
Washington Redskins

Central Division:
Chicago Bears
Detroit Lions
Green Bay Packers
Minnesota Vikings
Tampa Bay Buccaneers

Western Division:
Atlanta Falcons
Los Angeles Rams
New Orleans Saints
San Francisco 49ers

American Football Conference (AFC)

Eastern Division:
Buffalo Bills
Indianapolis Colts
Miami Dolphins
New England Patriots
New York Jets

Central Division:
Cincinnati Bengals
Cleveland Browns
Houston Oilers
Pittsburgh Steelers

Western Division:
Denver Broncos
Kansas City Chiefs
Los Angeles Raiders
San Diego Chargers
Seattle Seahawks

SUPER BOWL GAMES

1967: Green Bay, 35 Kansas City, 10
1968: Green Bay, 33 Oakland, 14
1969: N.Y. Jets, 16 Baltimore, 7

1970: Kansas City, 23 Minnesota, 7
1971: Baltimore, 16 Dallas, 13
1972: Dallas, 24 Miami, 3
1973: Miami, 14 Washington, 7

1974: Miami, 24 Minnesota, 7
1975: Pittsburgh, 16 Minnesota, 6
1976: Pittsburgh, 21 Dallas, 17
1977: Oakland, 32 Minnesota, 14
1978: Dallas, 27 Denver, 10
1979: Pittsburgh, 35 Dallas, 31
1980: Pittsburgh, 31
       Los Angeles, 19
1981: Oakland, 27
       Philadelphia, 10
1982: San Francisco, 26
       Cincinnati, 21

1983: Washington, 27 Miami, 17
1984: L.A. Raiders, 38
       Washington, 9
1985: San Francisco, 38 Miami, 16
1986: Chicago, 46
       New England, 10
1987: N.Y. Giants, 39 Denver, 20
1988: Washington, 42 Denver, 10
1989: San Francisco, 20
       Cincinnati, 16
1990: San Francisco, 55
       Denver, 10

FOOTBALL ORGANIZATIONS

For further information, contact these groups:

National Football League (NFL)
410 Park Avenue
New York, NY 10022
(212) 758-1500

National College Athletic
Association (NCAA)
Nall Avenue at 63rd Street
PO Box 1906
Mission, KS 66201
(913) 384-3220

National Federation of State High
School Athletic Associations
11724 Plaza Circle Box 20626
Kansas City, MO 64195
(816) 464-5400

Pop Warner Football
1315 Walnut Street Building
Suite 606
Philadelphia, PA 19107
(215) 735-1450

Further Reading

Illustrated Football Dictionary for Young People, by Joseph Olgin
     (Prentice Hall, 1975)
Be a Winner in Football, by Charles Coombs (Morrow, 1974)
30 Years of Pro Football's Great Moments, by Jack Clary (Rutledge
     Books, 1976)
The Story of Football, by Dave Anderson (Morrow, 1985)
Playing with a Football, by Morris A. Shirts and Thomas R. Kingsford
     (Sterling, 1973)
How to Play Better Football, by C. Paul Jackson (Crowell, 1972)

SCORE YOUR NEXT TOUCHDOWN WITH A NEW FOOTBALL!

25 Winners!

Enter the KNOW YOUR GAME SUPER FOOTBALL GIVEAWAY.

Win an impressive all-leather football. Just fill out the coupon below and return it by February 28, 1991.

Look for more great books in the KNOW YOUR GAME series. From football to baseball, these guide books give you sports tips and pointers so you can play like the pros.

Rules: Entries must be postmarked by February 28, 1991. Winners will be picked at random and notified by mail. No purchase necessary. Void where prohibited. Taxes on prizes are the responsibility of the winners and their immediate families. Employees of Scholastic Inc.; its agencies, affiliates, subsidiaries; and their immediate families not eligible. For a complete list of winners, send a self-addressed stamped envelope to Know Your Game Super Football Giveaway, Giveaway Winners List, at the address provided below.

Fill in the coupon below or write the information on a 3" x 5" piece of paper and mail to: **KNOW YOUR GAME SUPER FOOTBALL GIVEAWAY**, Scholastic Inc., P.O. Box 759, 730 Broadway, New York, NY 10003. Canadian residents send entries to: Iris Ferguson, Scholastic Inc., 123 Newkirk Road, Richmond Hill, Ontario, Canada L4C365.

- -

Know Your Game Super Football Giveaway

Name _____ Age _____

Street _____

City _____ State _____ Zip _____

Where did you buy this *Know Your Game* book?

❑ Bookstore ❑ Drugstore ❑ Supermarket ❑ Library

❑ Book Club ❑ Book Fair ❑ Other_____(specify)

KYG490